ANCIENT INVENTIONS

AHEAD OF THEIR TIME

Written by Teresa Turner

STECK-VAUGHN
A Harcourt Company

www.steck-vaughn.com

CONTENTS

INTRODUCTION

When we think of inventions, we often think of electric lights, telephones, and computers. These **devices** make our life easier and more comfortable. We push a button on a washing machine, and it cleans our clothes. We turn the key to a car, and it can take us hundreds of miles in only one day.

Just as we want an easier, better life, so did people of long ago. They needed fast ways to travel. They needed to know how much time had passed. They wanted to look their best and to enjoy life. How did ancient people solve these problems? They invented things. Today we call those inventions ancient. But to people of long ago, their inventions were ahead of their time.

CHAPTER 1
INVENTIONS FOR TRAVEL

How are modern times different from the past? One of the most important differences is our ability to travel long distances quickly. Inventions such as airplanes, cars, and high-speed trains allow us to move easily from place to place. We sometimes feel sorry for people who lived long ago. We think they had to walk or ride animals wherever they went, but they didn't. In fact, ancient people invented some clever ways to get around.

Skis and Skates

One of the oldest and best ways to travel on snow is to ski. The ancient people of Russia used skis. How do we know? Parts of a pair of very old skis have been found in the mountains of Russia. The tip of each ski is carved in the shape of an elk's head. These skis are 8000 years old! In Norway a rock carving made more than 4500 years ago shows a person skiing. The skier is using a pole to push himself along.

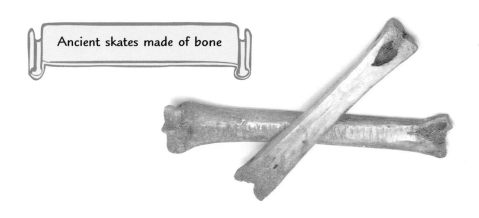

Ice skates came along a little later than skis. Early ice skates were made of bone and were shaped like little skis. To use the skates, people tied the bones to their shoes.

Carriages and Cars

In addition to skis and skates, ancient people also made carriages and cars. About 1600 years ago, a Chinese emperor wrote about a carriage with sails. This carriage could hold 30 people and go hundreds of miles a day. Of course, if the wind was not blowing, it would not go.

The Chinese also invented a carriage-like device that told how far a person had traveled. This invention was one of the first **odometers**. When one *li* (a Chinese measurement equal to $\frac{1}{3}$ mile or about 500 meters) had passed, a wooden figure on top of the carriage struck a drum. When ten *li* had been traveled, another figure struck a bell.

People in the northern part of China made special sail cars for traveling over ice. These sail cars had smaller wheels than the ones made for traveling on land. When people from Europe visited China in the 1500s AD, they saw sail cars being used. When they went back home, they made their own sail cars. These cars traveled at speeds up to 30 miles (48 kilometers) per hour.

A Chinese sail car

The calendar we use today was invented by people of the Christian religion. In this calendar the years are numbered by how far they are from the birth of Jesus Christ. The abbreviation *AD* stands for *anno domini* ("in the year of the Lord" in Latin). It follows the years after the birth of Christ. The years before Christ's birth are counted backward. The abbreviation *BC* stands for *before Christ.* It follows the years before the birth of Christ. The timeline above can be used to understand the dates mentioned in this book.

In 1425 a European man named Giovanni di Fontana wrote down some ideas for cars. In one of his ideas, the car worked a little like a top. The driver pulled a rope connected to the wheels. Pulling the rope made the wheels turn. This idea was not very practical.

In another of di Fontana's ideas, a rocket powered the car. A container attached to the car was filled with fuel made from **gunpowder**. The fuel exploded when it burned, making the car move forward. As far as we know, no one ever tried to build this dangerous car.

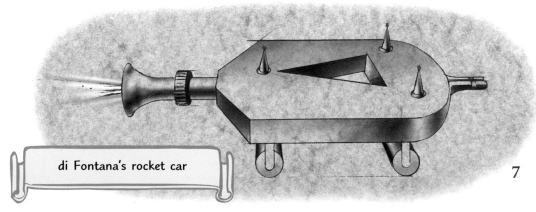

di Fontana's rocket car

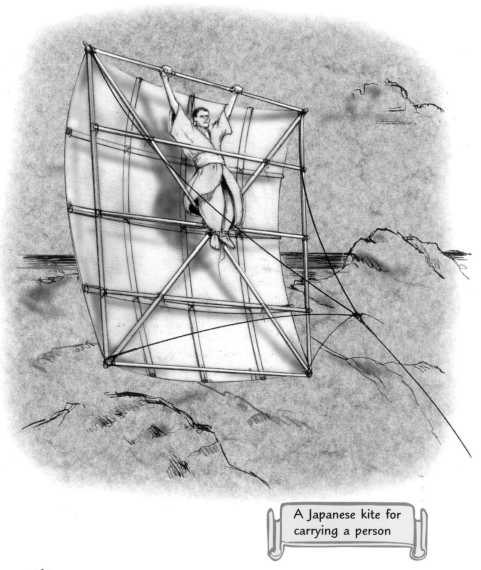

A Japanese kite for carrying a person

Kites

The Chinese also developed another great travel invention. They made a kite big enough to carry a person! When the Chinese were at war, they may have sent men up in kites to spy on the enemy.

The Japanese also made kites for carrying people. They probably used these kites when one of their cities was surrounded by an enemy army. The kites carried people past the enemy.

Compasses

Travel was sometimes hard for ancient people. In places without roads, getting lost was easy. Once people got lost, they had a hard time figuring out which way they were going and how far they had traveled.

The Chinese were the first to solve the direction problem. They invented the first compass. It didn't look at all like a modern compass. It didn't point north, and it certainly didn't fit in a pocket. In fact, it was a cart called the "south-pointing carriage." The figure of a man on the carriage pointed south. When the cart turned, the figure turned so that it always pointed south.

The south-pointing carriage was probably invented about 1700 years ago. How did it work? It contained a system of **precise** gears. The carriage had two wheels.

When it turned left or right, the wheel that had farther to go turned faster than the other wheel. The gears used this difference in speed to turn the figure at the top of the carriage.

The first **magnetic** compass was also invented in China. It was shaped like a spoon! In fact, it was called the "south-controlling spoon." The spoon was set on a special metal plate. It turned by itself so that the handle pointed south.

CHAPTER 2
INVENTIONS FOR TELLING TIME

Today many of us live our life according to clocks. Everywhere we go, we see clocks in towers, on walls, and on desks. Have you ever wanted to go back to a time before clocks? If you did, you might have to go back farther than you think.

Shadow Clocks and Water Clocks

Long ago the Egyptians made two kinds of clocks. The first were shadow clocks. The earliest shadow clock was probably a stick or pole stuck in the ground. The length of the pole's shadow gave some idea of the time of day. A later shadow clock looked like an L. It had a straight base and a raised crosspiece at one end. The shadow of the crosspiece told the time of day.

The second kind of Egyptian clock was the water clock. The Egyptians made this clock from a large cup or jar with a tiny hole in the bottom. The inside of the cup was marked with the hours of the day. As the level of the water in the cup dropped, the hour marks showed.

Shadow clocks could only be used during the day. Water clocks were more useful than shadow clocks because they could be used day or night.

Ancient Greeks and Romans also used both shadow clocks and water clocks. Their shadow

An Egyptian water clock

clock was the sundial. Unlike the Egyptian shadow clock, the sundial's shadow traced an **arc**. Sundials were usually made of wood or stone. The hour marks were arranged like the numbers on a modern clock face.

Ancient people in many parts of the world used sundials. This sundial is from ancient China.

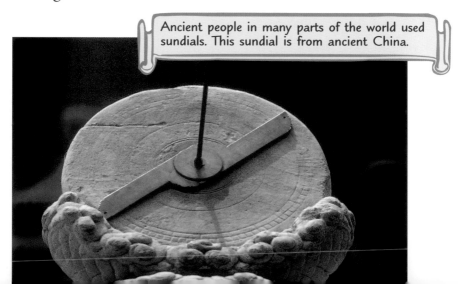

Some Greek water clocks were very large and beautiful. One clock rang bells, made puppets move, and made toy birds sing. The Greeks and Romans used small water clocks in their law courts. The water clocks were used to tell how long a person had been speaking, so that both sides could be given equal time. Water clocks were also used to time races. They showed just how fast the winners were.

One wonderful ancient Greek clock still stands and is called the Tower of the Winds. It was built about 2000 years ago. Figures that stand for the winds appear on the tower's eight sides. Two sides of the tower have sundials. Inside the tower sits a fancy water clock. Long ago the water clock showed the time on a dial.

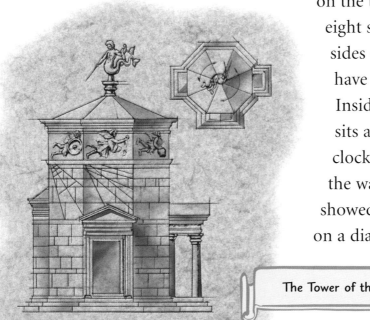

The Tower of the Winds

13

Mechanical Clocks

The first mechanical clock was invented by a Chinese person. It used water to move **machinery** made of bronze and iron. The inventor of this clock called it the "Water-Driven Bird's-Eye-View Map of the Heavens." This clock soon broke down.

A more successful mechanical clock was Su Sung's "Cosmic Engine." It also used water to move machinery. The front of the tower had five doors stacked on top of each other. On the hour, puppets came out of the doors. Some of them hit drums, bells, and gongs. Other puppets played musical instruments. This clock ran for more than a hundred years!

Early European clocks had weights and ropes. One famous clock was made in Italy around AD 1350. This clock showed the date, the hour, and the placement of the sun, moon, and planets. Another well-known clock had a mechanical rooster that stretched out its neck, flapped its wings, and crowed on the hour.

Most early clocks had only one hand. This hand showed the hour. Later, another hand was added to clocks to show the minutes. Finally, another hand was added to show the seconds.

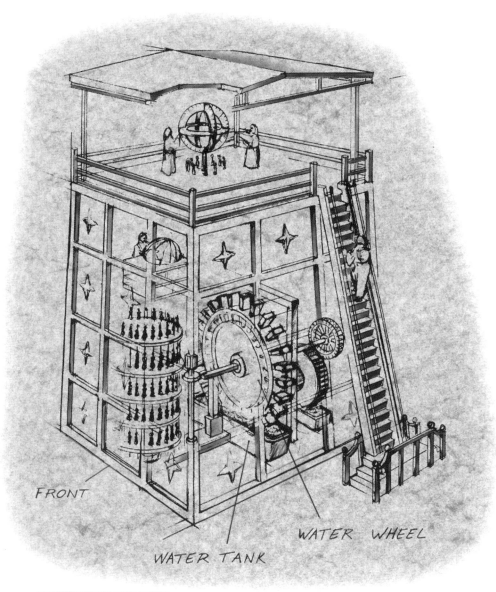

FRONT

WATER TANK

WATER WHEEL

The Cosmic Engine

Inside the lock were pieces of metal that stuck out. The key had gaps for these pieces to pass through. When the key turned, it pulled back the bolt. The metal pieces stopped a key that had gaps in the wrong places.

Ancient people also used **padlocks** and chains. Both the Chinese and the Romans invented their own types of padlocks. Long ago in Europe, shopkeepers used padlocks to protect their shops.

Earthquake Detectors

Throughout history, earthquakes have killed many thousands of people. Locks kept people's homes safe, but they couldn't keep out these natural disasters.

A Chinese man named Chang Heng invented an "earthquake weathercock." His machine, he claimed,

A modern seismograph

18

could **detect** earthquakes at a distance. Heng's machine was shaped like a barrel. The heads of eight dragons stuck out around the barrel's rim. Each dragon held a bronze ball in its mouth. Below each dragon sat a bronze toad. When the earth quaked, one of the dragons dropped its bronze ball into the mouth of the bronze toad below it. The ball made a loud clanging noise. The noise let people know that there had been an earthquake. The direction of the earthquake was opposite that of the dragon and the toad under it.

At first, people at the emperor's court didn't believe this invention would work. Then one day they heard a clang. No one had felt the earth move. Still, one of the dragons had let go of its bronze ball. Four days later, word came to the palace of an earthquake. It happened in the direction shown by the machine.

Chang Heng's earthquake detector

No one knows for sure how Heng's earthquake detector worked. Some scientists think that the middle of the detector held an upside-down **pendulum**. Tiny shock waves from an earthquake made the pendulum hit a piece of wood that ran through the dragon head. The piece of wood hit the ball and made it fall from the dragon's mouth.

Coding Devices

Ancient people sometimes had to defend themselves from their enemies. At times they needed to give secret orders to an army far away. How could they keep an enemy from reading them? The ancient Greeks used a simple invention called a *scytale* (SIT uh lee) to keep messages secret. First they made two poles of wood that were exactly the same size. One pole was given to the general leading the army. The other pole was kept by the person who sent messages to the general. When the person wanted to send a message, he wound a thin strip of paper around the pole. Then he wrote his message lengthwise on the paper. When he was done, he unwound the paper and sent it to the general. The unwound paper showed a scrambled series of letters.

The general wound the paper around his pole so he could read the message.

A later invention for keeping secrets was the **cipher** disk, invented in AD 1400. It was actually made of two disks. The larger disk was on the bottom. The smaller disk sat on top of the larger disk. Letters and numbers were written around the edges of both disks.

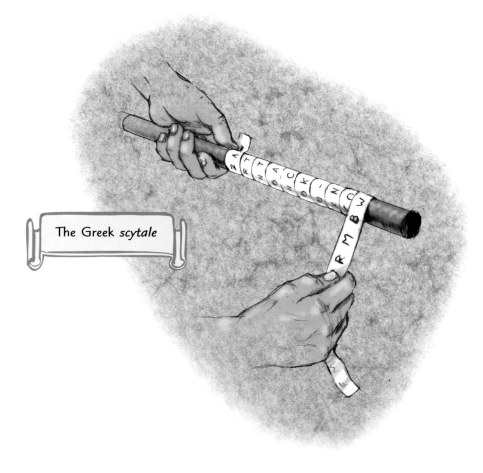

The Greek *scytale*

The cypher disk

To write a message, the user turned the inner disk so that its letters lined up with the ones on the outer disk. Then, for each letter on the inner disk, the user substituted the matching letter on the outer disk. At the beginning of the message, the writer gave a key letter pair. For example, if the pair was A = q, the person receiving the message turned his cipher disk so that A on the outer disk lined up with q on the inner disk. Then he replaced each letter from the outer disk with its mate on the inner disk.

CHAPTER 4
INVENTIONS FOR BEAUTY

We use many inventions to keep ourselves looking good. We take showers and use soap. We look in mirrors to see how we look. These things may seem very modern, but they were actually invented in ancient times.

Showers

The ancient Greeks invented showers. A painting on a Greek vase made about 2300 years ago shows women athletes taking a shower. The painting shows water running through overhead pipes and spraying out through shower heads shaped like the heads of boars and lions. A rod across the top of the shower holds towels and clothes.

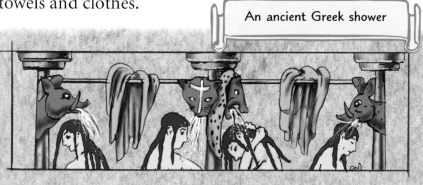

An ancient Greek shower

An ancient "magic" mirror and its reflection

The Chinese made the most amazing mirrors of the ancient world. These "magic" mirrors were made of bronze. One side was highly polished to show a reflection. The other side had a pretty design. When the polished side of one of these mirrors was held up in strong sunlight, the design on the other side appeared on the wall.

How could light pass through solid bronze? Scientists did not solve this mystery until AD 1932. Of course, light did not really pass through the bronze mirrors. The polished side actually had tiny **indentations** that matched the pattern on the back. These indentations were too small to be noticed. Because the polished side of the mirror was convex, the tiny indentations appeared on the wall as a larger design.

Make-Up

How much time did ancient people spend looking into their mirrors? Probably a lot. Like us, they looked into mirrors to arrange their hair and put on make-up.

The first known use of make-up happened in the Middle East. We know this because a little gold make-up kit shaped like a shell was found in an ancient burial tomb. This make-up kit is more than 4000 years old! Women of the Middle East lined their eyes with a black substance called kohl. Kohl was made from a **mineral** called antimony and from a kind of lead. Women also used dyes to color their cheeks.

The ancient Egyptians loved make-up. They often used powdered minerals called **ochres**. They rubbed yellow ochre into their skin to brighten it. A mixture of red ochre and fat was used on the cheeks and lips. To color their eyelids, they used either a blue mineral called lapis lazuli (LAP is LAZ uh lee) or a green one called malachite (MAL uh kyt).

An ancient Egyptian woman with her makeup kit

Egyptians carried their make-up in little leather bags. They ground the lumps of minerals into powder on special small boards. Then they used sticks of wood, glass, ivory, or bronze to paint the minerals on their skin.

The people of ancient India used a face cream made of white lead to lighten their skin. The use of this kind of make-up spread throughout the world. In later years Roman doctors discovered that make-up made of white lead was poisonous. Still, Roman women were determined to use it. One emperor's wife covered her face with white lead. She covered her body with white chalk. She painted her lips and cheeks red. Her eyelids, eyelashes, and eyebrows were painted black. She outlined her veins with blue paint. Today we would think she looked very strange.

False Beards

Some ancient fashions seem silly today. We wear wigs on our heads, but some ancient people also wore wigs on their chins! False beards were popular in several times and places.

Ancient Egyptians wore false beards because they thought real beards were ugly. Egyptian men shaved their faces carefully. Then they put on beards made of braided human hair or wool that was cut square at the bottom. Egyptian kings wore larger beards than those of other people. These big beards were an important symbol of royal power. Even Hatshepsut, a queen of Egypt, wore a false beard!

False beards were also popular in old France and Spain. Some people used them as disguises so that they could break the law. The problem was so serious that false beards were not allowed in France in the 1500s AD.

An ancient Egyptian ruler with a false beard

CHAPTER 5
INVENTIONS FOR FUN

Does anyone really need bubble gum, skateboards, and wind-up toys? These inventions are just for fun. Ancient people liked to have fun, too. Some of their inventions are still used today.

Chewing Gum

To find a pack of chewing gum today, you can walk into a store and find many different kinds and flavors. For people long ago, gum was harder to find.

The first people to chew gum were the ancient Greeks. They chewed gum made of sap from a certain tree. The Mayan people of Mexico invented chewing gum that is very much like the gum we chew today. They noticed that when they cut the bark of a sapodilla (SAP uh DEE yuh) tree, a thick liquid oozed out. The Mayans called this liquid *chicle* (CHEE klay). When the liquid hardened, it made a tasty gum. Chewing gum was very popular in the Mayan Empire.

In AD 1866, some chicle was brought to an inventor named Thomas Adams. At first he tried to turn the chicle into something like rubber, but it wouldn't harden. But Adams agreed that chicle made good chewing gum. He added flavorings and sweeteners to make the first modern chewing gum.

Fireworks

When you see fireworks on the Fourth of July, thank the ancient Chinese. They invented fireworks. The first firecrackers were made from pieces of bamboo closed at both ends. The bamboo was thrown into a fire. The fire heated the air inside, and the bamboo exploded with a bang!

After they invented gunpowder, the Chinese made many kinds of fireworks. They added chemicals to turn the fireworks different colors. They put metal shavings in some fireworks to make them sparkle.

The Chinese also made moving fireworks called water rats and ground rats. These fireworks moved rapidly across the ground or water, trailing flames behind them. The water rats even moved on little water skis!

Fireworks came to India in AD 1200, but they didn't make it to Europe until AD 1500. Europeans then used fireworks to celebrate holidays much as we do today.

Puppet Theaters

People in all times and places have enjoyed puppets and **marionettes**. A brilliant inventor named Heron of Alexandria made one of the most amazing puppet shows ever.

Fireworks in modern China

Heron's puppet theaters worked without the help of people. No one had to touch them. One of Heron's theaters looked like a little building set on a column. It rolled forward by itself. Then it opened its doors. Wooden puppets performed a short play. Then the doors closed, and the theater rolled back to where it started.

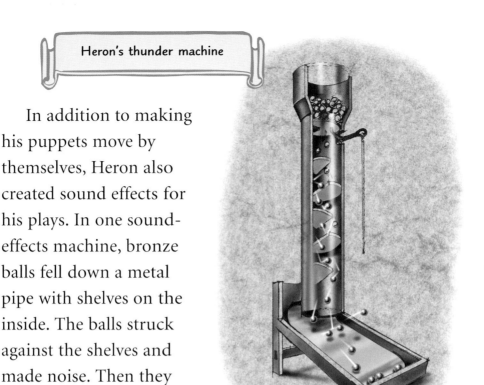

Heron's thunder machine

In addition to making his puppets move by themselves, Heron also created sound effects for his plays. In one sound-effects machine, bronze balls fell down a metal pipe with shelves on the inside. The balls struck against the shelves and made noise. Then they fell out of the bottom onto a sheet of tin. The result was the sound of thunder.

Musical Instruments

Before the theater was invented, people enjoyed music. The oldest musical instrument is the flute. Flutes more than 15,000 years old have been found in Europe and Russia. These flutes are made of bone.

The bull-roarer is another very old instrument. A bull-roarer is a flat piece of wood or stone shaped a bit like a fish. A string is tied through a hole in one end.

When the bull-roarer is whirled around the player's head, it makes a loud noise. Bull-roarers about 14,000 years old have been found in Germany and Denmark.

The ancient Egyptians made an odd rattle called a sistrum. The sistrum had a metal loop with a long handle. Three or four holes were drilled on each side of the loop. Wires with rattles were threaded through the holes. When shaken, the sistrum made a sound like the wind blowing through reeds.

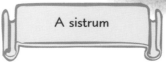

A sistrum

CHAPTER 6
INVENTIONS TO IMPRESS

Have you even been impressed by a beautiful car or a glass elevator? People have always wanted to impress others.

Water Dispenser

The ancient Greeks especially wanted to impress people in their temples. Before entering a temple, people had to wash their hands and face. Heron of Alexandria built a coin-operated water **dispenser** to be used outside temples. The water dispenser looked like a large, fancy jug. The customer put a coin in a slot at the top of the jug. The coin fell onto a lever. The lever opened the valve on a **spigot,** and water came out. When the lever had tilted enough, the coin fell off. The lever moved back up and shut off the water.

Heron also invented **automatic** doors for temples. When a person lit a fire on an altar outside the temple, the doors slowly opened. After the fire went out, the doors closed again.

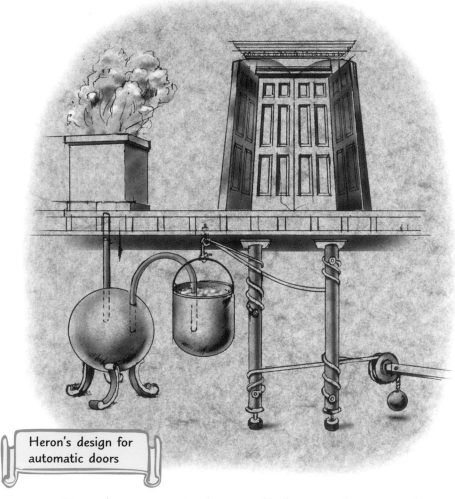

Heron's design for automatic doors

Heron's automatic doors relied on underground machinery. When the fire was lit, a pipe beneath it brought hot air into a round metal container of water. As the water heated, it spilled out into another pipe. This pipe emptied into a bucket. As the bucket got heavier, it pulled chains wound around long rollers attached to the doors.

Floating Statues

If people weren't already impressed with a temple's coin-operated water dispenser and automatic doors, they surely were when they went inside. In at least two ancient temples, a large, solid statue appeared to float in the air! These statues were made of magnetic stone. Powerful magnets hidden in the temples' roofs and walls held the statues in place.

A floating statue

Glossary

arc (ARK) a curved line

automatic (aw tuh MA tik) working by itself

cipher (SY fuhr) a code

convex (kon VEKS) curved outward

detect (dih TEKT) to find out about, to discover, to notice

devices (dih VYS iz) things that are made by people to be used for a certain purpose

dispenser (dis PEN suhr) a machine that gives out something in small amounts

distorted (dis TAWRT id) twisted out of shape

gunpowder (GUN pow duhr) a powder that explodes when set on fire

imported (im PAWRT id) brought in goods from another country for sale or use

indentations (in den TAY shuhnz) notches or grooves

machinery (muh SHEE nuh ree) the working parts of a machine

magnetic (mag NET ik) having a great power to attract

marionettes (mair ee uh NETS) puppets that are controlled from above by strings or wires attached to their arms and legs

mineral (MIN uh ruhl) a natural solid material that is found in the earth

ochres (OH kuhrz) yellow and red dirt made of iron

odometers (oh DAHM uh tuhrz) instruments that tell how far vehicles have traveled

padlocks (PAD loks) locks that can used on doors, gates, lockers, or chains

pendulum (PEN dyuh luhm) a weight that swings back and forth on a string or wire

precise (pruh SYS) exact; having the proper order or details

seismograph (SYZ muh graf) an instrument that shows when and where earthquakes happen

spigot (SPIG uht) a faucet

tumbler (TUM bluhr) the part of a lock that makes the bolt move when a key is turned

INDEX